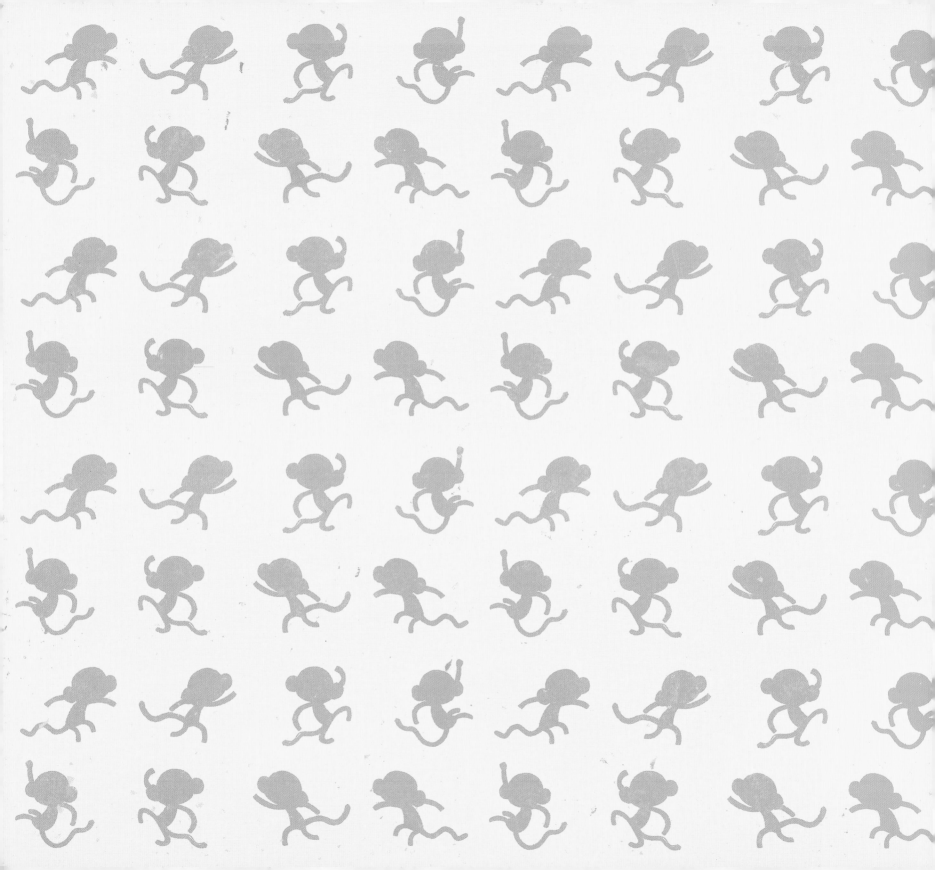

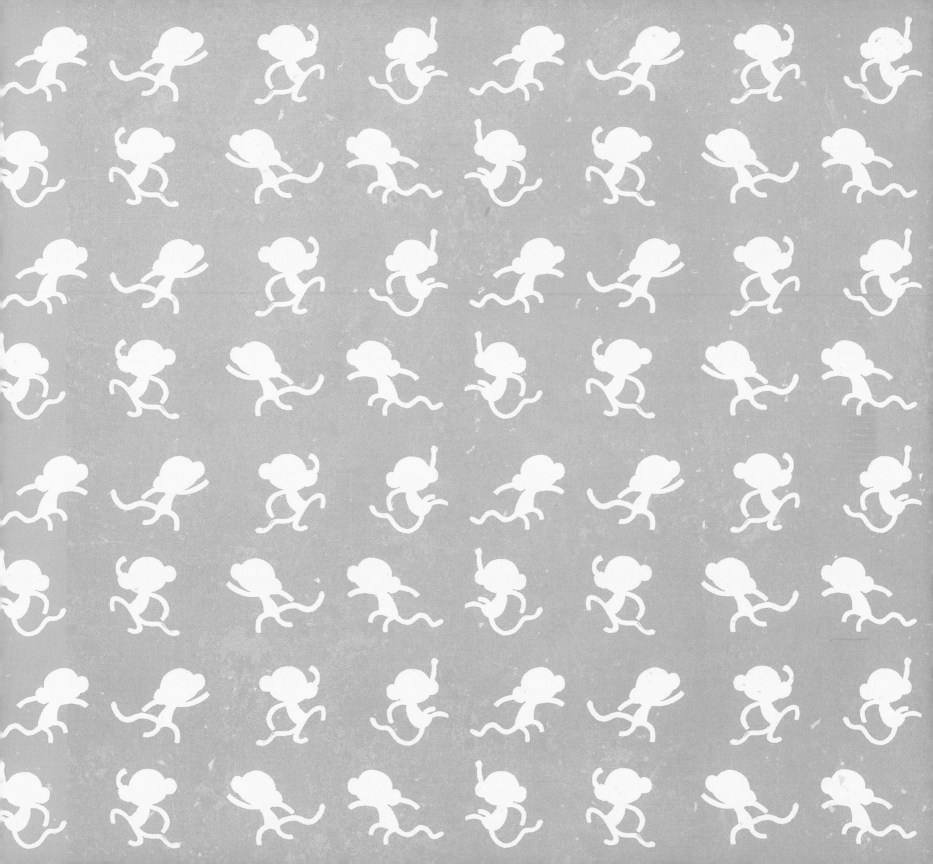

For my parents, Una and Christo, with love – Bridget

For my parents, Sheila and Jeff – Steve

First published in 2010 by
Futa Fata,
An Spidéal,
Co. na Gaillimhe,
Ireland,
under the title *Lúlú agus an Oíche Ghlórach*

This English-language edition © 2013 Futa Fata
Original text © 2010-2013 Bridget Bhreathnach
Illustrations © 2010-2013 Steve Simpson

Adapted from the original Irish by the author

ISBN: 978-1-906907-76-1

Futa Fata

www.futafata.ie

Lulu
and the
Noisy Night

written by
Bridget Bhreathnach

illustrations by
Steve Simpson

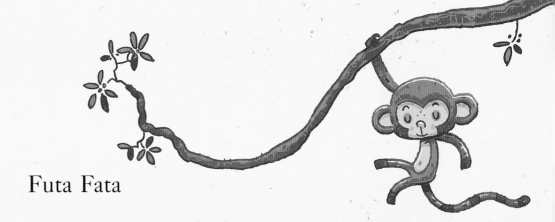

Futa Fata

Lulu, the little monkey, was very happy in her big tall tree, in the middle of the forest. She lived with her Mommy and Daddy and lots and lots of brothers and sisters. Above them, on the highest branch of the tree lived Lulu's very best friend – Jackie the Owl.

All day long, Lulu loved to play in the branches:

Jumping.

Swinging.

Running.

And Dancing.

But at night, things were different.
One by one, all of the monkeys
would fall asleep.

All of the monkeys — except Lulu.

She lay on her branch, listening to the strange sounds of the forest.
Somewhere below, she heard a **"RARR RARR!"**.
Then a **"TRUMP TRUMP!"** Further away, she heard a
"CROAK CROAK!" And then, the scariest noise of all —
a long, low, **"HUUU HUUUU!"**

At the top of the tree, Jackie the Owl was watching her little friend.
She stretched out her long wings and glided down silently.
"What's the matter, dearie?" she asked as she landed on the branch.
'The forest is so noisy!" said Lulu. "It's scary and I can't sleep."

"I've an idea!" said Jackie. "Why don't you come for a ride with me? We'll soon find out where all those noises are coming from." So Lulu climbed onto Jackie's back and away they flew, into the moonlit night.

They hadn't gone very far when Lulu heard a noise that gave her a scare
"RARR RARR!" she heard, **"RARR RARR!"**

"Do you hear that big, rough noise?" asked Lulu.
"Oh Jackie, I don't like this. I want to go home!" she said.

Rarr!
Rarr!

Rarr!
Rarr!

"But look, Lulu," said Jackie. "It's just a Daddy Lion playing with his little son before he puts him to bed". **"RARR RARR!"** said the little lion as he laughed with his Daddy, **"RARR RARR!"** "Oh Jackie," said Lulu, "they're having such fun!"

"Let's keep going," said Jackie,
"to see what we can see."
Up they flew into the sky,
high above the forest.

Before long they came to a big wide river,
glistening below them in the moonlight. Just then,
Lulu heard another scary noise.
"TRUMP TRUMP!"
she heard,
"TRUMP TRUMP!"

Trump!
Trump!

Trump!
Trump!

"Did you hear that big, scary noise?" asked Lulu.
"Oh Jackie, I don't like this. I want to go home!"

"But look, Lulu," said Jackie. "It's just a Mommy Elephant giving her baby a bath before she goes to bed."

"TRUMP TRUMP!" went the baby elephant, laughing happily. **"TRUMP TRUMP!"**

"Oh Jackie," said Lulu,

'The elephants are having fun too!"

"Let's keep going" said Jackie, "to see what we can see."
Up they flew into the sky, high above the river.

Jackie and Lulu continued along the river until they came to a wide lake, shimmering calmly in the moonlight. Just then, Lulu heard another noise that gave her a scare. **"CROAK CROAK!"** she heard. **"CROAK CROAK!"**

"Did you hear that strange, croaky sound?" said Lulu.
"Oh Jackie, I don't like this. I want to go home!"

"But look Lulu," said Jackie. "It's just Daddy and Mommy frog singing with their little baby before he goes to sleep." **'CROAK CROAK!'** said the baby frog as he sang happily with his Mommy and Daddy. **'CROAK CROAK!'** "Oh Jackie," said Lulu, "They're having such fun."

"We should be getting back home now," said Jackie. "It's time for a certain little monkey to go to sleep!" Up they flew into the sky, high above the lake.

Silently they flew across the moonlit sky, all the way back to Lulu's tree. When they arrived, Mommy, Daddy and all of the little monkeys were still asleep. Just then, Lulu heard a noise high up above them. **"HUU HUUUU!"** she heard, **"HUU HUUUU!"**

Huuu
Huuuu!

"Oh Jackie, I'm afraid."

"But Lulu – that's my Mommy! She comes here to visit me every night."
"Your Mommy!" said Lulu, laughing. **"HUU HUUU!"** said Jackie,
as she flew away into the night **"HUU HUUUU!"**

"Thank you, Jackie!' Lulu called softly.
Then the little monkey lay down happily
and closed her eyes.

All around the monkey's big tree
the forest was still full of noises.

'RARR RARR!'
went the lions

"TRUMP TRUMP!"
went the elephants

'CROAK CROAK!!'
went the frogs

And **'HUUU HUUU!'**
went the owls.

But Lulu the little monkey didn't hear a thing. She was fast asleep.

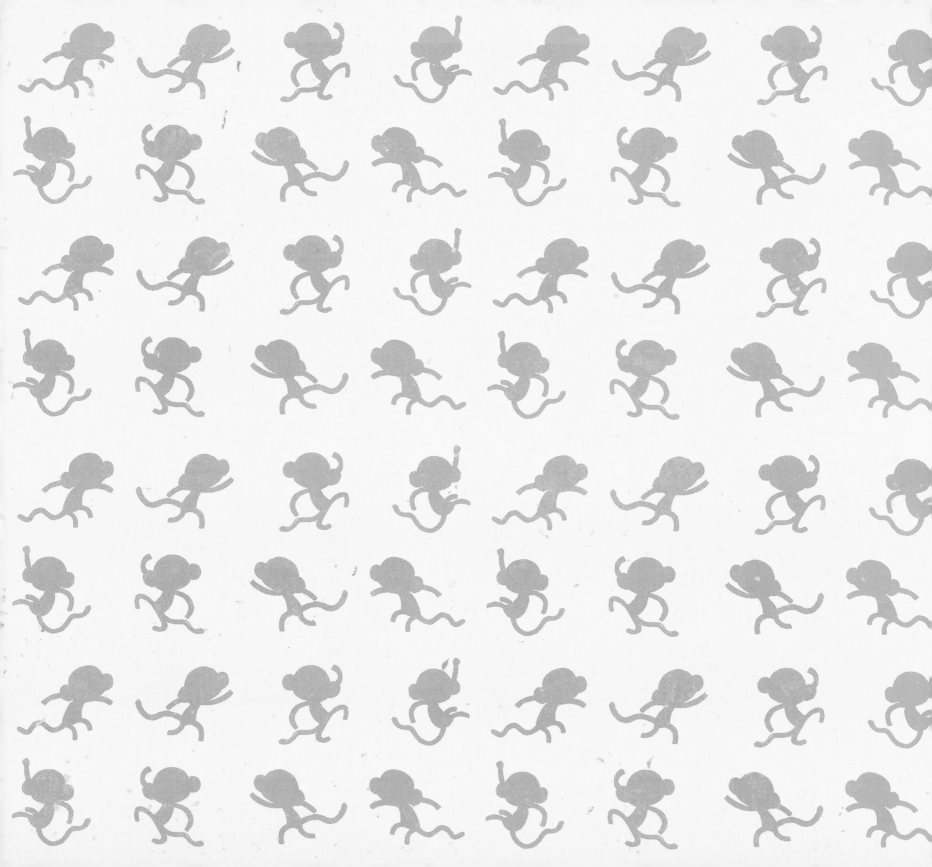

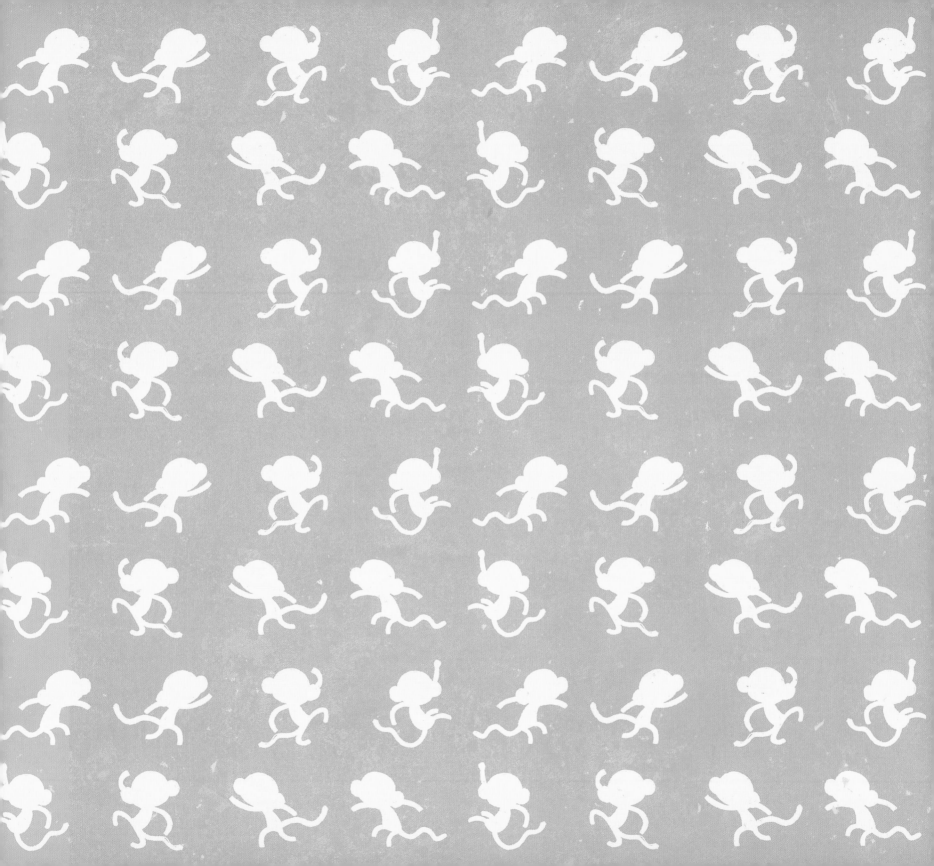